ADVENTURES

—AT—

HOUND HOTEL

PICTURE WINDOW BOOKS
A Capstone Imprint

Adventures at Hound Hotel is published by Picture Window Books,
A Capstone Imprint
1710 Roe Crest Drive
North Mankato, Minnesota 56003
www.capstoneyoungreaders.com

Library of Congress Cataloging-in-Publication Data
Sateren, Shelley Swanson, author.
Mudball Molly / by Shelley Swanson Sateren; illustrated by Deborah Melmon.
pages cm. — (Adventures at Hound Hotel)
Summary: Twins Alfie and Alfreeda are charged with getting Molly the West Highland
white terrier fully groomed in time for her owner's wedding, where she will wear a
collar bearing the wedding rings—the trouble is that Molly hates being groomed and
has apparently buried the collar somewhere at the Hound Hotel.
ISBN 978-1-4795-5900-8 (library binding)
ISBN 978-1-4795-5904-6 (paperback)
ISBN 978-1-4795-6194-0 (eBook)
1. West Highland white terrier—Juvenile fiction. 2. Kennels—Juvenile fiction.
3. Twins—Juvenile fiction. 4. Brothers and sisters—Juvenile fiction. 5. Wedding
rings—Juvenile fiction. [1. West Highland white terrier—Fiction. 2. Dogs—Fiction.
3. Kennels—Fiction. 4. Twins—Fiction. 5. Brothers and sisters—Fiction.
6. Weddings—Fiction.] I. Melmon, Deborah, illustrator. II. Title.
PZ7.S249155Mu 2015
813.54—dc23   2014026590

Designer: Russell Griesmer

Printed in China.
092014   008473RRDS15

Mudball Molly

by Shelley Swanson Sateren
illustrated by Deborah Melmon

TABLE OF CONTENTS

ADVENTURES AT HOUND HOTEL

IT'S TIME FOR YOUR ADVENTURE AT HOUND HOTEL!

At Hound Hotel, dogs are given the royal treatment. We are a top-notch boarding kennel. When your dog stays with us, we will follow your feeding schedule, give them walks, and tuck them in at night.

We are always just a short walk away from the dogs — the kennels are located in a heated building at the end of our driveway. Every dog has his or her own pen, with a bed, blanket, and water dish.

Rest assured . . . a stay at the Hound Hotel is like a vacation for your dog. We have a large play yard, plenty of toys, and pool time in the summer. Your dog will love playing with the other guests.

HOUND HOTEL
WHO'S WHO

WINIFRED WOLFE
Hound Hotel is run by Winifred Wolfe, a lifelong dog lover. Winifred loves dogs of all sorts. She wants to spend time with every breed. When she's not taking care of the canines, she writes books about — you guessed it — dogs.

ALFIE AND ALFREEDA WOLFE
Winifred's young twins help out as much as they can. Whether your dog needs gentle attention or extra playtime, Alfreeda and Alfie provide special services you can't find anywhere else. Your dog will never get bored with these two on the job.

WOLFGANG WOLFE
Winifred's husband pitches in at the hotel whenever he can, but he spends much of his time traveling to study wolf packs. Wolfgang is a real wolf lover — he even named his children after pack leaders, the alpha wolves. Every wolf pack has two alpha wolves: a male one and a female one, just like the Wolfe family twins.

Next time your family goes on vacation, bring your dog to Hound Hotel.

Your pooch is sure to have a howling good time!

CHAPTER 1
Total Shaggy Mess

I'm Alfie Wolfe, and there's one thing I hate. Getting groomed! *Ugh!*

I hate getting my hair cut or even brushed. And getting dirt and junk dug out of my ears and fingernails? Yuck.

I really hate getting it done proper-like by my mom. It hurts, it's boring, and it takes forever. It's the worst!

A few weeks ago, I met a dog that hated getting groomed even more than I do, if you can believe that. Her name was Molly. Molly the West Highland white terrier.

White? Ha. Not even close. When I first met her, she didn't even look like a Westie. (That's the nickname for that kind of terrier.)

Westies are pure white after they're washed. But Molly wouldn't go anywhere near a bathtub, so she was the color of dirt.

She wouldn't let anyone near her with a hairbrush or scissors. So she was a total shaggy mess too. I couldn't even see her eyes.

I'll tell you the whole story about Molly

the little mudball. Maybe you're saying, "Who cares? So what if some dog didn't want her hair washed and chopped off? Who does?"

Well, it turned out that somebody had a lot to lose if Molly didn't get groomed like a show dog.

That somebody was *me*.

❁ ❁ ❁

It all started on a Friday. The day had started out normal. At about seven o'clock, I banged on my dog-shaped alarm clock to make it stop barking.

I leaped out of bed and raced to get ready for school. I had to beat my sister, Alfreeda. She makes everything into a contest. See, she always acts like alpha kid around our place. Top dog in every way. The fastest. The smartest. The strongest. The bravest. It drives me crazy!

But that day I had her beat in two departments: dressing and grooming.

At alpha-guy speed, I grabbed jeans and a Hound Hotel T-shirt off my floor and tugged them on. I dashed to the bathroom and bumped Alfreeda away from the mirror.

"Hey, cut it out!" she yelled.

Before she even had a chance to shove me back, I rubbed my teeth with a finger of toothpaste. I gave it one good rub. Then I ran my fingers through my hair. It just took one fast tug.

"Done," I said and jumped to the doorway. "Beat you!"

Alfreeda rolled her eyes.

"Alfie," she said in her tired-teacher voice. "When will you ever get it? Mom will just make you do it again. Or she'll take over and do it, since you're so helpless. Like she always does."

I crossed my eyeballs at Alfreeda. "Doubt it," I said.

"Don't doubt it," she said.

Suddenly I saw two sisters standing in front of me. No one needs two sisters! So I uncrossed my eyeballs and flew downstairs.

In about four seconds flat, I poured a bowl of cereal and headed for the kennel building. It's at the end of our long driveway, past the apple trees and chicken coop.

I wolfed down my breakfast on the way. I don't waste time with spoons, not when I can be playing with dogs down at the kennels. And I only got a little milk on my shirt. Okay, a lot.

I threw open the office door and yelled, "Mom! I'm up and ready!"

"Oh, good. Come here, Alfie," she called from down the hall. Her voice sounded even more cheerful than normal.

I headed through the office, past the laundry room, and past the storeroom. She was all the way back in the grooming room.

The grooming room has a table that moves up and down, depending on the size of the dog. We have a big washtub for the baths. Next to the tub is a shelf with tons of dog shampoos and lots of Hound Hotel towels.

And then there are the grooming tools. Mom puts on her finishing touches with shavers, clippers, and blow-dryers.

"Is the Westie here yet?" I asked.

"No," Mom said and smiled at me. "Molly will be here when you get home from school."

"Did any other dogs check in?" I asked.

"Not yet. More are coming around dinnertime." Mom patted the dog-grooming table. "Hop up, Alfie."

I groaned, long and *loud*. "Not today, Mom," I said. "You always do this to me."

"Well, honey, today it's even more important that you look your very best," she said in a voice that sounded like some bird singing in the springtime. It made me very suspicious.

So I whirled around and bolted for the door.

— CHAPTER 2 —
Good Enough!

"Not so fast, bud," Mom said. She grabbed my arm. Gentle-like, but firm.

Mom's got some strong muscles. She's lugged around a lot of big dogs for a lot of years. She's always lifting them in and out of the washtub and on and off the grooming table.

She picked me right up and plopped me onto the table, like I weighed no more than a teensy Chihuahua.

Mom grabbed a dog brush. It was the big kind that can handle big grooming jobs on big furry dogs. The brush had my name on it. Mom always used it on my fur.

She started to tug through my mop of hair. To be honest, I've got poodle-like hair. (Alfreeda does too.) It's super thick and curly and crazy. Combs don't work. Really, only dog brushes can do the job.

"Come on, Mom." I groaned again. "It's Friday. Even the teachers dress down on Fridays. Who cares what I look like?"

"Calm down, Alfie," Mom said. She pulled a dead ladybug out of my hair. She dropped it next to the little piles of burrs she'd already tugged out.

Then she started to brush. And brush. Then she brushed some more.

She wouldn't stop! She was going totally overboard!

"That's good enough," I complained. "Stop."

"Relax, Alfie," Mom said. Finally, she dropped the brush onto the table. But then she grabbed some scissors.

"What?" I cried. "I don't need a haircut!"

"Alfie, you haven't looked this shaggy in months," she said. "Now sit still, please, so I can do this right."

I knew what that meant. *Right* meant *perfect*. See, my mom's a pro dog groomer. The best around. She always made our hotel guests look great before they went home. She was famous for that.

Sometimes I think Mom forgets I'm a kid and not a canine. I wasn't supposed to look perfect.

Now I couldn't wiggle or anything. Not with scissors pointed at my head. I sighed loud and heavy.

"This is the worst part," I said. "Sitting still, forever and ever. How long is this going to take?"

Mom smiled. Then she said in that singsongy, springtime robin voice, "If you miss the school bus, I'll drive you to town."

"What?" I cried. "Mom, why is it so important that I get a haircut right now?"

"Well, honey," she said in a sugar-loaded voice, "you know my friend from high school, Primrose? Her family owns the food market in town?"

"Sure," I said. "The world's tiniest grown-up. She can't pat me on the head anymore. I'm as tall as she is now. What about her?"

"She's getting married tomorrow," Mom said. "Right in her parents' backyard in town. Isn't that exciting?"

"No," I said. "So what?"

"Well," Mom cleared her throat and went on, "Primrose and her husband-to-be, Harry, adopted a little Westie named Molly two months ago. Primrose wants Molly to be the flower girl in her wedding. Isn't that sweet?"

"No," I said.

Mom chewed her lip and started to trim my bangs.

"Get to the point, Mom," I said.

"Okay, Alfie!" Mom snapped and chopped off half my bangs. I looked around the room. Wow, I could see stuff with my left eyeball. Nice and clear. Not like I was looking through a dirty curtain anymore.

"Let me explain," Mom said. "See, Molly won't let anyone groom her. Not Primrose, not Harry, no one. Primrose says I'm her last and only hope. She wants Molly looking like a Westie show dog in time for the wedding tomorrow. The wedding starts at two o'clock. But Molly should look like a show dog for the

21

rehearsal tonight. At the very latest, she needs to be ready for photos at ten tomorrow."

"What's that got to do with me?" I asked.

"Well, see, Alfie," Mom went on, clipping away at my hair, "it sounds like Molly is afraid to be groomed. She's young, only about three years old. Maybe her first owner never groomed her, so Molly's afraid of it now. Or maybe that owner was too rough with Molly during brushing and bathing. Who knows?"

"The point?" I asked.

"Settle down, Alfie," Mom said. "I told Primrose I'd try to groom Molly beautifully by tomorrow. But I said I didn't have high hopes. It can take weeks of slow, calm, gentle training to turn a dog's grooming fears around. I told Primrose that she needed a back-up plan for flower girl. So . . ."

"Yeah?" I said.

"Well, Alfie," Mom said, "I offered your services to Primrose. As back-up flower kid."

"What?" I yelled and leaped off the grooming table.

── CHAPTER 3 ──
Shaved Right Off

I blasted out of the kennel building and up our driveway, all the way to our country road. That's where the school bus picks up Alfreeda and me.

I bolted up the trunk of the old maple tree by the road. I climbed to a top branch and held on tight.

Mom's a fast runner. She's built up powerful legs over the years, chasing after runaway dogs.

She peered up
the tree trunk.

"Alfie, come
down," she said.
"Please listen."

"No," I said.
"I don't want to
be flower kid
or flower dog or
flower anything! Let
her do it!" I pointed
at Alfreeda.

She headed over with
her backpack, ready
for school. "Let me do
what?" she asked.

Then she looked
at me and started to
laugh her head off.

"What did you do to your hair?" she cried. "Wow! I'd hide in a tree too. For the rest of my life!"

Slowly, I reached up and rubbed my fingers over my head, the whole top of it.

A thick furry helmet covered half of my head. The other side was shaved right off, from the top of my forehead to the back of my neck.

My heart started to pound.

Alfreeda looked at Mom. "What's he talking about?" she asked. "Let me do what?"

Quick, Mom explained the problem.

"Why did you say Alfie would do it?" Alfreeda cried. "Why not me? I would have so much fun, throwing flower petals all over the place. Everyone would take pictures of me. I'd get to eat all that wedding cake. Why didn't you tell Primrose I'd do it?"

"Because Primrose is so tiny," Mom said. "The flower kid can't be taller than she is. But she doesn't know any little kids, except Alfie."

"I'm *not* little, Mom!" I shouted.

"Yeah!" Alfreeda cried. "We're the same height!"

"So why me?" I yelled. "I hate weddings! And how come you always make me get my hair cut? Why not her? She crawls around in the fields and chases after dogs as much as I do. She gets burrs and dead bugs in her hair. How come you only groom me, huh?"

Mom didn't even have a chance to answer.

"Because, Alfie," Alfreeda said, "I brush my hair twice a day. *And* I do a top job every time. You never do."

She had a point.

I stared at my sister and realized something: she looked as groomed as a show dog. She had big, puffy, perfect hair, loaded with ribbons. Not a burr or dead bug anywhere. Her face and hands and fingernails had a soap-and-water shine. Even her teeth sparkled.

How does she do that? I wondered. *Without help from Mom or anything?* Suddenly I realized my sister was alpha kid in the grooming department.

That's fine, I thought. *Let her have the honor.*

"Okay, kids," Mom said. "This is the deal. Alfreeda, you have big tall hair. It adds inches to your height. Also, you have a very nice habit of standing up straight."

"Thanks, Mom," Alfreeda said.

Mom looked at me. "But you, Alfie?" she said. "You always walk around with your shoulders all caved in, sagging toward the ground."

She paused and slouched to show me how I walk. "No matter how many times I tell you to stand up straight, you don't," Mom said. "I can count on you. I just know you'll stand all bent over during Primrose's wedding. You won't outsize the bride."

Suddenly, Alfreeda's shoulders caved in. She put her hands on top of her head and squashed her hair flat.

"Please, Mom?" Alfreeda begged. "Tell Primrose I'll do it. If I'm flower girl, I bet they'll let me have seconds at cake time."

"Great idea!" I cried. I leaped out of the tree and landed on the grass with a thud.

I patted my sister on the shoulder then jumped in front of Mom. I stretched my backbone way out. I stretched my neck as far as it could reach, too. I even stood on tiptoe. My nose almost touched Mom's nose.

"Sorry, Alfie." She shook her head. "I bet the second you head down that garden path, tossing rose petals, you'll forget all about standing up straight. It's settled, Alfie. I'll try, but I doubt Molly will let me groom her. So, you're back-up flower kid. Just take a bunch of deep breaths. It'll be over before you know it."

"*Aarg!*" I growled. Sometimes it was just useless arguing with my mom!

"No fair," Alfreeda complained. "I bet they'll give Alfie thirds at cake time."

Suddenly the school bus roared up.

I dragged my feet up the bus steps behind Alfreeda.

The bus was full of kids. They were talking

real loud, like always. But the second I stepped inside, everybody shut up.

Right away, fingers started to point at my head. A bunch of mouths fell open and started to laugh like crazy.

I spun around and flew off the bus.

CHAPTER 4
Who's This Movie Star?

Mom made me super late for school that morning.

At about eleven o'clock, she finally finished the grooming job.

I got totally groomed, from the top of my head down to my toenails. Even my teeth sparkled.

She made me put on a clean Hound Hotel T-shirt too.

"There, handsome," she said and grinned at me. "We. Are. Done. You look like a prize-winning show dog. All that's missing is the white dress shirt, pressed pants, and a tie."

I was so disgusted, I couldn't even talk.

Mom drove me to school and kept saying, "So handsome! Who knew?"

She parked outside the school and said, "Now, Alfie, stay clean at recess and all afternoon. Tonight, after the groom's dinner, the wedding party is going to practice the wedding, in Primrose's parents' rose garden. That means you too."

She had to be kidding me. I couldn't stay clean that long! I banged the car door shut and didn't even say goodbye.

I headed into my classroom and no surprise, my teacher didn't even recognize me.

"Well, who's this movie star?" Ms. Ruff whispered to me.

I think some kids heard her. Anyhow, everybody stared. My friends looked at me sad-like and said, "Sorry, dude."

I ran to my desk and wished I could wear a baseball cap at school to keep my head covered.

Right then, I made a rock-solid decision: I would *never* again, in my *whole* life, let *anybody* groom me. For sure *not* my mom!

Now I knew exactly how that little terrier Molly felt. *My mom better not force her to get groomed*, I thought. *No dog should have to suffer like this.*

Suddenly, I made another firm decision: I'd make sure that Alfreeda would get the flower-kid job. And I knew just how to do it.

I told Alfreeda my plan on the bus ride home. We shook on it.

We got off the bus and saw a real tiny yellow car parked in our driveway. "That must be Primrose's car," Alfreeda said.

"Figures," I said. "Let's go."

We raced inside and upstairs to the attic. We dug through bunches of boxes and piles of junk, searching for the stuff we needed.

Alfreeda grabbed a straw hat covered with fake flowers out of the costume box. "Perfect," she said.

She dropped it on the floor and jumped on it about ten times to flatten it. Then she put it on her head. Dead-looking flowers hung over the rim. A couple of long ribbons hung down on either side too.

Alfreeda tied the ribbons tight under her chin. The hat squashed her hair super flat.

"Great!" I said. "How about this?"

I grabbed a tall top hat from the costumes and put it on.

"Wow," Alfreeda said. "You look almost as tall as Dad!"

Then I stuck my feet into some man-size dress shoes. They had super-thick heels.

"Cool!" Alfreeda said. "Now you tower over me! Don't forget to stand up super straight when Primrose shows up."

"Okay," I said. "And don't forget to cave your shoulders way in."

"I won't." She flew down the attic stairs. About two seconds later, I heard the kitchen door bang shut.

I'm proud to say I tripped only four times on the stairs. We've got a lot of stairs in our big old farmhouse.

Finally I got outside and dragged those boat-size shoes toward the kennel building.

I made it halfway there when the hairiest man I ever saw came out of the office door.

A furry rocket blasted around him. It flew down the front steps and shot straight at me.

"Molly!" the man called. "Come back!"

The furry dirtball barked her shaggy head off at me. It sounded like this: *errr-RWOW! Errr-RWOW!*

Molly sprang up and dug her super-long toenails into my ribs. I shot backward. My shoes and hat flew off. I landed on my rear end in the middle of the driveway.

"Alfie!" the man cried. "You are Alfie, correct? The back-up flower kid? I was coming to find you. Are you okay?"

"I don't know." I groaned.

CHAPTER 5
Strike a Deal

I sat up, good and slow, and checked a few bones.

Nothing seemed to be broken. "I'm think I'm fine," I said. "I'm used to rowdy dogs."

Molly wagged her tail like crazy and tried to lick my face. Usually, I'm okay with that. But I pushed Molly away. She had real bad breath.

"Man, you need your teeth brushed," I said. "*Ugh.*"

She hopped away and put her head deep inside the top hat, like it was a rabbit hole or something.

The hairy man grabbed my hand and helped me up. Even his hands were hairy.

He had long, shaggy hair and a bushy beard. He was even hairier than my dad when he gets home from a long wolf-study trip in the wilderness. (That's my dad's job. He's gone a lot, studying wolf packs Up North.)

The weird thing was the hairy man wore a fancy suit.

He shook my hand and said, "I'm Harry."

"I can see that," I said.

He threw back his head and laughed. "Everyone makes that mistake," he said. "My *name* is Harry. H-A-R-R-Y."

"Oh." I laughed. "Got it. Look, Harry, are you the guy who's marrying Primrose? Because I really don't want to be flower kid."

"I didn't figure you did," he said. "It was nice of you to offer."

"I didn't!" I said. "My mom signed me up."

"*Hmm.*" He rubbed his bushy chin. "Truth is, I hate getting my hair and beard cut, too. Primrose has begged and begged me to get them trimmed before the wedding. But my guess is, if Molly gets groomed, Primrose will be so happy, she'll forget about shaggy old me. Can I strike a deal with you, Alfie my man?"

"Sure," I said. "What?"

"If you help your mom make Molly look like a true Westie, I'll pay you twenty dollars."

"Wow!" I said and whistled.

"Here's the catch," Harry said. "You have to make sure that Molly's neck and beard are trimmed short."

"Why?" I asked.

"So this will show!" He pulled a skinny dog collar out of his suit-coat pocket. It had tiny yellow roses on it. Two shiny gold rings hung from it. "Our wedding rings!"

Then Harry whistled with his fingers and Molly dashed over.

He pulled her shaggy hair away from her neck and

put the collar on. As he buckled the collar in place, he explained.

"You see, Alfie," he said, "Molly will be the flower girl *and* the ring bearer in our wedding tomorrow."

"The ring what-er?" I asked.

"The ring bearer. That means she'll carry the rings to Primrose and me during the wedding," he said. "I'll whistle, she'll come running, and Primrose will be so surprised to see the beautiful rings on Molly's neck."

"Cool," I said. "Don't worry. I won't tell anybody. It'll be a great surprise."

Harry grinned. "So, my friend, can Molly get groomed in time for the rehearsal dinner?"

"You bet," I said, and we shook on it. *For twenty bucks?* I thought. *For sure!*

"Wonderful." Harry started to dig in his suit-coat pockets. "I'll even pay you up front. Now, where did I put my money clip?"

He checked and double-checked all his pockets. Then he triple dug, and his eyes got real wide and frightened-looking.

About then Molly took off running, down the driveway, chasing a couple of robins.

Harry started to shout, "Where's my money clip? Where did I leave it this time? I had all the money for the groom's dinner clipped together. The dinner starts in half an hour! Where on earth is my money? Oh, no!"

He dashed to the office door, threw it open, and called for Primrose.

She ran outside, and they had a fast, whispered talk. Right then I realized that Primrose actually looked like the flower she was named after. She wore a yellow flowery dress and matching hat.

"Your money clip?" she cried. "You lost your money clip. Oh, Harry, not again! We have to go find it!"

They dashed to the little yellow car and jumped inside. Harry started the engine.

"We'll see you at the rehearsal," Primrose called to Mom. "I can't wait to see my Molly looking beautiful. If anything can cheer me up, that will!"

And the teensy car zoomed away.

CHAPTER 6

Backed into a Corner

Mom looked at her watch. "It's hopeless, kids," she said. "I can't groom Molly in less than three hours."

"Of course you can't," Alfreeda said. "Please, Mom, ask Primrose if I can be flower kid . . ."

I grabbed Mom's arm and pulled her inside the kennel building. I led her to the grooming room.

"Get the supplies ready, Mom," I said. "I'll go get Molly. If anybody can make that mudball

look like a million bucks, it's you. You're
a pro!"

"Well, thank you, Alfie," Mom said with
a smile.

I dashed out the front door to find Molly. I
was going to make sure I got my twenty bucks.

I finally found her out back. I couldn't
believe my eyeballs! Somehow, she'd gotten
into the dogs' play yard, behind
the kennel building. Molly was
busy digging a deep hole in
the middle of the yard.

"Hey, how'd
you get in
there, girl?"
I called.
"The gate is
locked."

Then I noticed a hole under the fence. It hadn't been there before.

"Wow, Molly," I called. "You're the alpha digger — the speediest around!"

I climbed over the fence and picked her up. "You're even dirtier now," I said. "But no problem. Mom will clean you right up."

I carried her to the play-yard door and through the kennel building. *This is going to be the easiest twenty bucks I've ever earned*, I thought.

Inside, Mom shut the grooming-room door behind us. Some quiet, peaceful song played on the MP3 player.

Mom laid a dog brush on the floor. She put a doggie treat beside the brush. Gentle-like, I set Molly near them.

"Yum," I said. "Go get the tasty treat."

Molly didn't even look at the snack. She stared at the hairbrush and started to cry. She backed into a corner.

I grabbed the brush and said, "It's okay, Molly. See? It's not sharp or anything." I moved the brush toward her.

Mom said, "Alfie, no."

Too late. Molly started to shiver and cry even louder.

Mom took the brush and dropped it in a drawer. "We just can't rush this, Alfie," she said. "Come here, Molly. It's okay."

Mom kneeled down and put a treat on the floor. Molly smelled it. Then, real slow, she ate it.

"Come here, honey." Mom pulled Molly onto her lap. "If you were brushed every day, little girl, it wouldn't be so painful. Your hair gets filled with knots when you don't let people brush it. That's what makes combing hurt."

Mom tried to run her fingers through Molly's hair. She leaned over and looked close at Molly's skin.

"Oh, no," Mom said. "Your skin is sore, Molly. This must be very uncomfortable for you! I bet it's driving you crazy, isn't it? You should be bathed every week, at least. With a dog shampoo for skin problems. Oh, yes, we've got to get you better."

Mom gave Molly another treat. This time Molly wolfed it down.

"Would you at least let me brush your teeth today?" Mom asked her. "You know, if you don't let people brush your teeth, you could become a very sick little dog. Some bad things could start to happen, even in other parts of your body."

Suddenly I didn't care about the twenty dollars. I just wanted to get Molly healthy.

"Can I help?" I asked.

"Sure," Mom said. "Grab a dog brush and the dog toothpaste. She'll like the flavor."

Right that second, Alfreeda ran into the grooming room. "Mom!" she said. "Primrose and Harry are back! They just drove up."

"Oh, I wonder if they forgot something," Mom said.

Suddenly Harry came tearing down the hall. He ducked his head inside and looked right at Molly.

"Oh, good," he said, out of breath. "There she is. Is she wearing the collar?"

"Huh?" Alfreeda said.

Harry winked at me and said, "You know, Alfie. The special collar?"

"Oh, right," I said. I kneeled down and felt around Molly's neck. I dug deep under the long, shaggy hair. It was filled with knots and bits of food and dirt.

"Mom," I said. "Did you take off Molly's collar?"

"No." Mom shook her head. "I don't think she was wearing one."

"It's gone!" I cried.

CHAPTER 7
What Terriers Do Best

Harry looked as scared as a rabbit trapped by a terrier. Even his bushy beard trembled.

Primrose ran into the grooming room and stared at him.

"What's going on now, Harry?" she asked. "We should be at the groom's dinner! I'm sure everyone is waiting for us."

Harry took a deep breath and explained everything. He told her about the collar, the rings, the surprise. "But I guess I didn't put the collar on properly," he said. "It must've fallen off her."

Primrose slapped her hand over her mouth.

Suddenly Harry pointed at Alfreeda and me. "As soon as I find my money clip, I'll pay twenty dollars to the kid who finds those rings!" he said.

"Wow," Alfreeda said and looked at me. "Twenty dollars! Game on! I'll check the driveway." She dashed toward the front door.

"I know where the collar might be," I said. "Come on, everybody."

I dashed to the play yard. Everyone else tore after me.

"Molly just dug that hole," I said and pointed at the fence. "Maybe the collar dropped into the dirt." Then I pointed toward the middle of the play yard. "Molly just dug that hole too."

"Which one?" Harry asked. "There are so many out here."

"Um, I'm not sure," I said, looking around. Harry was right. There were holes all over the play yard.

"We've had lots of terriers stay at Hound Hotel lately," Mom said. "They're just doing what terriers do best: dig."

Suddenly Primrose whirled around and said, "Alfie, I need a rake and shovel please."

"Follow me," I said.

I led her to the garage. Super quick, we filled my old red wagon with shovels, rakes, and piles of gardening tools.

We pulled the wagon to the play yard. Everyone was on their knees now, Alfreeda too. Their fingers combed through grass, dirt, and small rocks. Molly was digging a new hole.

Before long, the whole wedding party showed up at Hound Hotel. Primrose had decided to call off the dinner and wedding practice. She wanted everyone to help search for the rings.

The men threw off their fancy suit coats. The women kicked off their high heels. Everybody got busy digging and raking and combing through dirt with their fingers.

"Where could those rings be?" cried Primrose.

Soon more of Harry and Primrose's family and friends showed up to help. Molly and three other Hound Hotel guests helped dig too. Holes and piles of dirt covered the playground.

At about eight, the sun set then clouds covered the stars. It started to rain. It was just a sprinkle. But it was enough to turn the dirt into mud and the workers into mudballs.

"Let's take a break and have something to eat," said Harry's dad. "We have a cooler full of sandwich fixings and lemonade."

After all that digging, everyone was starving. We dug into the food without even washing up.

The maid of honor sipped her lemonade and yawned. "Maybe we should call it a night," she suggested.

"No!" Primrose cried. "I'm *not* leaving this doggie play yard until we find those rings!"

Everyone gathered around her. "We'll keep searching, Primrose," said Harry.

"We can even set up some tents for rests," Mom offered.

So Harry and I set up every pup tent we could find in the attic. We made tents out of blankets, too. They covered the farmyard.

Then Harry and I got back to digging. I used every bit of alpha-kid strength I had. I kept rubbing dirt out of my eyes and thinking, *I'm going to find those gold rings. Any minute now, I'll be twenty bucks richer.*

We all kept digging until midnight. Then everyone crawled in the pup tents and slept.

Early the next morning, we got right back at it.

CHAPTER 8
A True Westie

Molly wasn't groomed in time for the pictures. But no one else was either. Primrose called off the photos. "We can't take pictures looking like this," she said. "Keep digging!"

So we kept moving piles of dirt around and around.

At noon, Primrose's mom begged her to stop the search. "Everyone needs to get clean and dressed for the wedding," she said.

"No," said Primrose. "We can't quit yet. I'm

not leaving this play yard without those rings. We'll just have the wedding right here!"

Harry took Primrose's hand and asked, "Are you sure? You wanted Molly and I to look perfect, and now no one looks perfect. Well, except you. You always look perfect to me."

"Oh, Harry," Primrose said with a sigh. "I'm sure. Maybe how we all look isn't as important as I thought. We can still have a wedding filled with love, even if everyone's covered in mud!"

She made some phone calls, and soon the pastor arrived in an old pickup truck. Then some flower people swept in with roses, ivy, and a fancy metal stand.

At two o'clock, Harry and Primrose stood in front of the roses, on top of a pile of dirt. They faced each other and held hands. Primrose looked like a spring flower in her yellow dress. A mud-splashed one.

The rest of the wedding party lined up in rows. I threw rose petals all over the play yard, and Molly chased them. She tried to bite them right out of the air, like they were birds or moths or dragonflies. It was actually pretty fun.

When the petals were gone, I stood with my empty basket on one side of the pastor, next to the groomsmen.

Alfreeda stood on the other side of the pastor, next to the bridesmaids. She held a little Hound Hotel doggie pillow. Harry had pinned an IOU to the top. The little piece of paper said:

My dear Primrose,
IOU one wedding ring.
love, Harry

Everyone else sat in the play yard, wherever there wasn't a big hole. Nobody had taken time to get washed up. Nobody had done their hair fancy or changed into fancy clothes.

The pastor faced Harry and Primrose. He started to say a bunch of stuff about marriage. Suddenly the crowd started oohing and ahing. People pointed at the rose-and-ivy stand.

I looked up. Two robins sat in the roses, right above Harry's and Primrose's heads. The robins sat side by side, their heads touching.

"Ah," said the pastor. "Love birds."

Suddenly Molly started to bark her head off at the robins. The birds took off flying toward the chicken coop.

The pastor got back to his speech. But I kept watching the robins. They landed on the chicken coop roof. I noticed a nest up there.

I stared at it. Something sparkled in the bright sunshine. My heart started to beat fast.

I reached around the pastor and poked Alfreeda. Then I pointed at the nest.

Her eyes got as big and round as a Westie's.

In about twenty seconds flat, we dashed through the play-yard gate and to the garage. We needed a stepladder.

We leaned it against the chicken coop. "I'll do it," I said before Alfreeda had the chance. I scaled the ladder at alpha-guy speed.

Right away, the robins flew to the other side of the roof. They chirped at me, loud and angry-like.

"Don't worry," I said. "I won't hurt your babies."

Four things lay at the bottom of the nest:

two blue eggs and two gold rings. Very carefully, I took the rings out of the nest. I didn't touch the eggs at all. And I left Molly's collar. It was twisted into the nest, between straw and grass and wildflowers.

"Found them!" I cried. I leaped off the ladder and ran back to the crowd.

Everybody cheered. I gave the rings to Harry. He shook my hand real hard, then Alfreeda's, and cried, "I knew I could count on you kids!"

I looked at my sister. A big grin covered her muddy face.

I grinned back and whispered, "I'm not taking money from a guy who keeps losing his money clip."

"Me neither," she whispered. "Who cares anyhow? Did you see the size of that cake?"

I nodded. "Sure did. Can't wait."

So Harry and Primrose got back to getting married.

Not long after they said, "I do," they cut the cake. Alfreeda and I both had thirds. And Molly had the biggest piece of all. Now she had yellow lemon cake all over her face too.

"We'll get you cleaned up, Moll, old girl," I said.

"Yeah, when Harry and Primrose are on their honeymoon," Alfreeda said. "We'll be really gentle, Molly, you'll see. Pretty soon, getting groomed won't be scary anymore. You'll look like a true Westie when your mom and dad get back."

Molly barked and wagged her tail.

"Hey," I said. "We should decorate the honeymoon car!"

"Yeah!" said Alfreeda. "Come on, Molly. You can help."

Before long, we had the little yellow car all decorated. We wrote "JUST MARRIED" on the windows with bars of dog soap. We tied empty dog-food cans from the back bumper.

Mom took a picture of the car, with everyone standing around it. The whole messy, muddy wedding party, with Molly right smack in the middle. Her pink tongue hung out of her mouth. And her tail wagged so fast it blurred in the picture.

That night, Alfreeda and I taped the picture over the dog-grooming table. It would be our "before grooming" snapshot of Molly.

Then we got the holes filled in the play yard.

That is, until Molly dug them out again.

Is a West Highland Terrier the Dog for You?

Hi! It's me, Alfreeda!

I bet you want your own cute, little, adorable Westie now too, right? I don't blame you. Westies make great pets for families! I mean, most families. But before you dash off to buy or adopt one, here are some important facts you should know:

Westies are big on barking. So if you've got a little baby at your house who needs to sleep a lot, get a pet rabbit instead. Barking is a Westie's way of saying she's happy or nervous or bored. If you DO get a Westie, don't yell when she barks. Yelling just makes dogs bark more! Stay calm and say "no bark" in a quiet voice. Give her a treat when she stops.

Westies LOVE to chase anything that runs away from them: mice, rabbits, squirrels, kids. The faster another animal runs away, the faster a Westie will chase it. When this happens, a Westie won't listen to its owner. So Westies HAVE to be on leashes or in a fenced-in yard to stay safe outside.

Westies need lots of attention. If they're left alone too long, they'll get bored and lonely, then they'll bark, dig, and chew things. So if you're the kind of family that's always gone at work and school and soccer games and music lessons, don't get a Westie. Get a goldfish.

Okay, signing off for now . . . until the next adventure at Hound Hotel!

Yours very factually,

Alfreeda Wolfe

VISIT
HOUND HOTEL
AGAIN WITH
THESE AWESOME
ADVENTURES!

Learn more about the people and pups of Hound Hotel
www.capstonekids.com

ADVENTURES AT HOUND HOTEL

Fearless Freddie

WRITTEN BY
Shelley Swanson Sateren

ILLUSTRATION BY
Deborah Melmon

ADVENTURES AT HOUND HOTEL

Homesick Herbie

en

ILLUSTRATION BY
Deborah Melmon

ADVENTURES AT HOUND HOTEL

Growling Gracie

WRITTEN BY
Shelley Swanson Sateren

ILLUSTRATION BY
Deborah Melmon

About the Author

Shelley Swanson Sateren grew up with five pet dogs — a beagle, a terrier mix, a terrier-poodle mix, a Weimaraner, and a German shorthaired pointer. As an adult, she adopted a lively West Highland white terrier named Max. Besides having written many children's books, Shelley has worked as a children's book editor and in a children's bookstore. She lives in Saint Paul, Minnesota, with her husband, and has two grown sons.

About the Illustrator

Deborah Melmon has worked as an illustrator for over 25 years. After graduating from Academy of Art University in San Francisco, she started her career illustrating covers for the *Palo Alto Weekly* newspaper. Since then, she has produced artwork for over twenty children's books. Her artwork can also be found on giftwrap, greeting cards, and fabric. Deborah lives in Menlo Park, California, and shares her studio with an energetic Airedale Terrier named Mack.